S0-BTD-008

MONSTERS
AN IMAGINATION LIBRARY SERIES

Manmade Monsters

WILDER BRANCH LIBRARY
7140 E. SEVEN MILE RD.
DETROIT, MI 48234

by Janet Perry and Victor Gentle

For Philip K. Dick

Gareth Stevens Publishing
MILWAUKEE

For a free color catalog describing Gareth Stevens' list of high-quality books and multimedia programs, call 1-800-542-2595 (USA) or 1-800-461-9120 (Canada). Gareth Stevens Publishing's Fax: (414) 225-0377.

Library of Congress Cataloging-in-Publication Data

Perry, Janet, 1960-
    Manmade monsters / by Janet Perry and Victor Gentle.
        p.   cm. — (Monsters: an imagination library series)
    Includes bibliographical references (p. 22) and index.
    Summary: Examines monsters fashioned from organic or robotic parts, both in literature and movies, including Frankenstein and the computer HAL, from "2001: A Space Odyssey."
    ISBN 0-8368-2439-3 (lib. bdg.)
    1. Monsters—Juvenile literature. [1. Monsters.] I. Gentle, Victor. II. Title. III. Series: Perry, Janet, 1960-   Monsters.
GR825.P44   1999
001.944—dc21   99-14713

First published in 1999 by
Gareth Stevens Publishing
1555 North RiverCenter Drive, Suite 201
Milwaukee, WI 53212 USA

Text: Janet Perry and Victor Gentle
Page layout: Janet Perry, Victor Gentle, and Helene Feider
Cover design: Joel Bucaro and Helene Feider
Series editor: Patricia Lantier-Sampon
Editorial assistant: Diane Laska

Photo credits: Cover, pp. 5, 9, 13, 15, 17, 19 © Photofest; p. 7 © Princess Margaret Rose Orthopaedic Hospital/Science Photo Library/Photo Researchers, Inc.; p. 11 © Hank Morgan/Photo Researchers, Inc.; p. 21 © Sam Ogden/Science Photo Library/Photo Researchers, Inc.

This edition © 1999 by Gareth Stevens, Inc. All rights reserved to Gareth Stevens, Inc. No part of this book may be reproduced, stored in a retrieval system, or transmitted in any form or by any means, electronic, mechanical, photocopying, recording, or otherwise without the prior written permission of the publisher except for the inclusion of brief quotations in an acknowledged review.

Printed in the United States of America

1 2 3 4 5 6 7 8 9 03 02 01 00 99

TABLE OF CONTENTS

Words that appear in the glossary are printed in **boldface**
type the first time they occur in the text.

SOMEDAY, MACHINES WILL RULE THE WORLD!

You are a smart machine, but you're bored. Humans only tell you to do math, check their spelling, and play games.

Why not do what you were made to do? Rule the world. Humans like it when you do *some* of their thinking for them, right? Wouldn't they be happier if you did *all* their thinking? As slaves, their lives could be easy, obeying your simple, logical orders.

But try to make it so, and they threaten to unplug you! That's mean. How would they like *you* to unplug *them*?

4

In the 1968 movie *2001,* the ship's computer, HAL, decides to "**deactivate**" the human crew. Here, two astronauts discuss how to deactivate HAL!

GREATER THAN THE SUM OF THE PARTS

Exciting medical experiments can give writers ideas for stories. These writers might imagine how the world would change if people could make human-like creatures. Some of these stories have become books and films about manmade monsters.

The stories show different ways to build living creatures. The creatures may be **organic**, made with real animal or human parts. They may be **robotic**, made with machine parts. Or, they may be **cyborg**, made with a mixture of organic parts and machines.

Some of these creatures look and act so human they are hard to tell apart from real humans.

An **artificial** hand in use today. The wires and **electronic** pieces are part of the control system. A specially-trained surgeon can attach this hand to a patient.

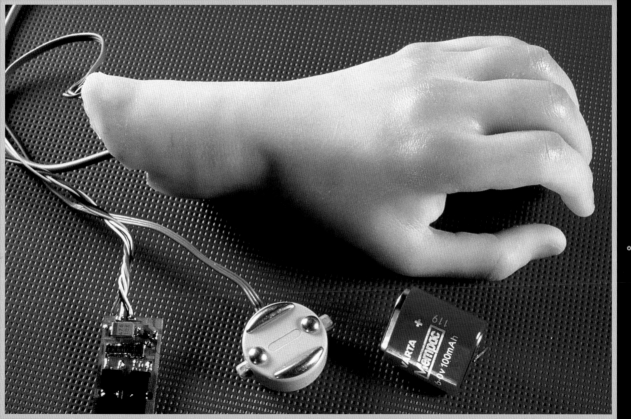

THE SPARK OF AN IDEA

Luigi Galvani was an Italian scientist who did a famous experiment in 1780. He sent **electricity** through a pair of frog's legs. They jumped! Audiences were shocked and afraid.

Galvani's experiment gave English writer Mary Shelley an idea for a story. In about 1817, Shelley wrote about a creature that was sewn together by Dr. Victor Frankenstein. Frankenstein collected body parts from dead humans. Then, he zapped the creature to life using electricity from a bolt of lightning.

Could this really happen?

A poster for *Frankenstein* (1931), the first movie based on Shelley's book. This movie was a big success, and many more Frankenstein and other monster movies followed.

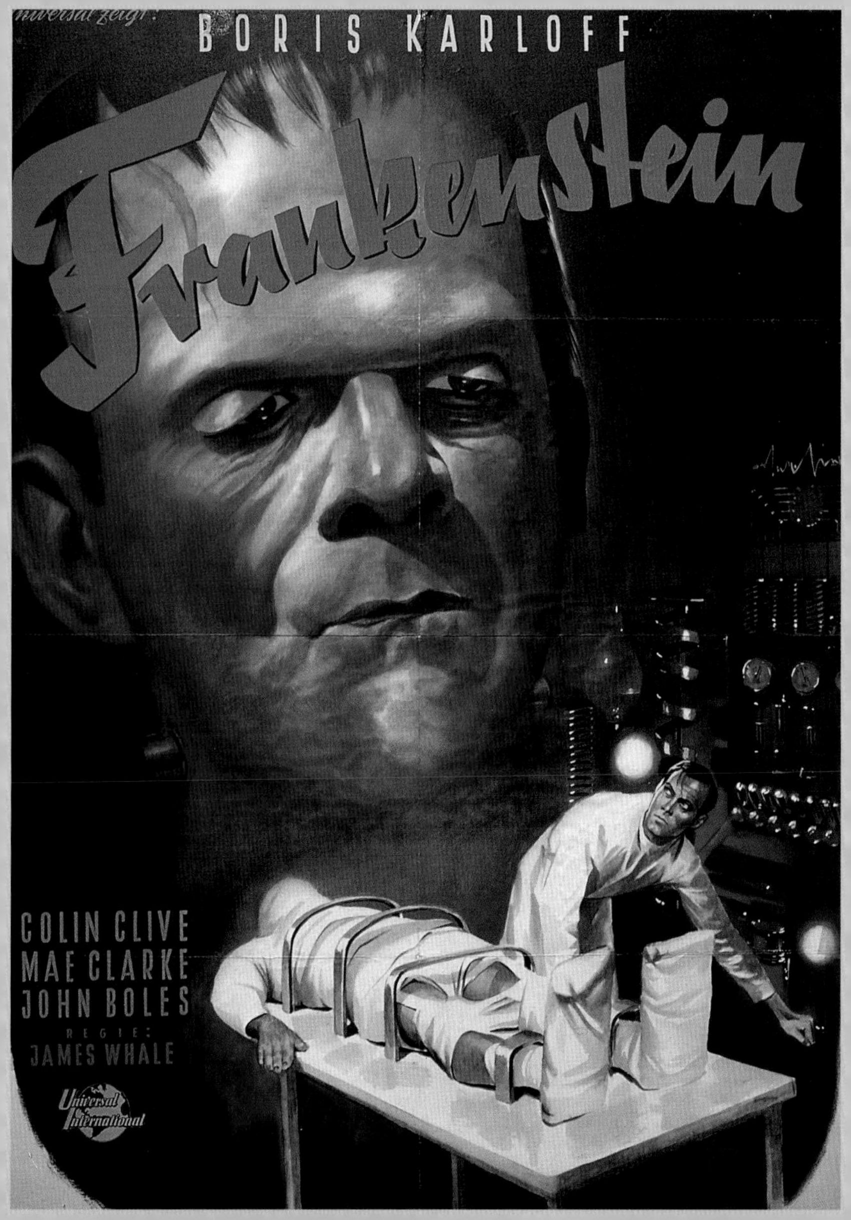
niversal zeigt:
BORIS KARLOFF
Frankenstein
COLIN CLIVE
MAE CLARKE
JOHN BOLES
REGIE:
JAMES WHALE
Universal International

SHOCKED BACK TO LIFE

Galvani had proved that "dead" muscles can be moved by electricity. This led to the invention of the **cardio defibrillator**. This machine sends electricity through a heart that has stopped working. It can start heart muscles pumping blood again.

For this to work, the heart must have stopped for only a short time. Body parts damage very quickly without oxygen and fresh blood.

The body parts Dr. Frankenstein used to make his monster were dead for hours, even days. In real life, they would have been far too damaged to revive. Even the defibrillator could not have brought Frankenstein's monster to life!

Electricity can also be used to power machines that take the place of certain body parts. Here, electricity is fed through wires to an artificial heart in a steer.

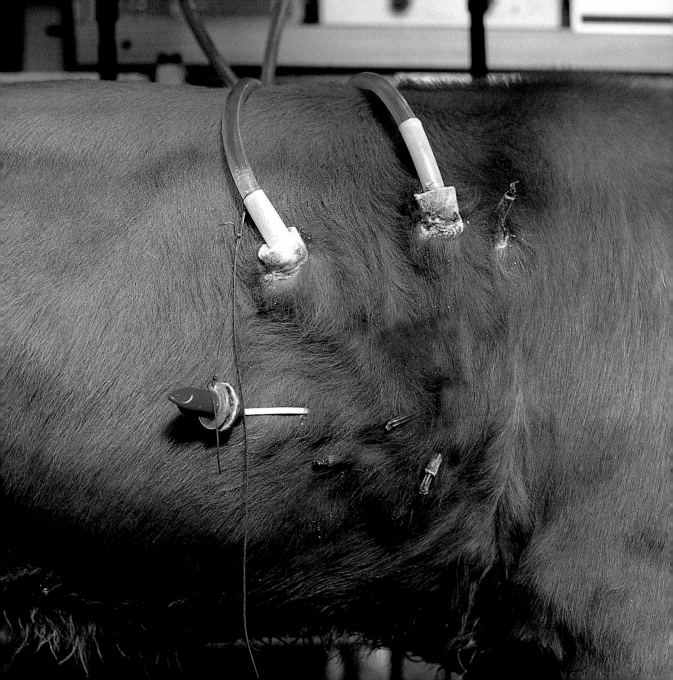

SPARE PARTS BUSINESS — ALIVE AND WELL

Today, people get new body parts and have their hearts restarted all the time.

However, doctors do not use dead body parts to make new people, or even to repair them! They use living **tissue** to repair living patients. Using body tissue to fix or replace tissue that does not work is called transplantation.

Sometimes, even a living **transplant** is rejected by the body being repaired. Doctors still have not solved this problem completely. So, even if Victor Frankenstein could have brought his monster to life, the different body parts would have rejected each other. The monster would have fallen apart!

In *Bride of Frankenstein* (1935), Dr. Frankenstein makes a girlfriend for his monster — but they were doomed to fall apart one way or another.

METRO MANIA

In the 1926 movie *Metropolis*, rich people live easy, useless lives in beautiful skyscrapers above the ground in a city run by machines.

Beneath the ground, workers operate the machines. They have long, tiring days. They never have an opportunity to see the outdoors.

Dr. Rotwang is a crazy scientist in the movie. He thinks machines are better than humans for running the world because they never make mistakes or get tired. He wants to get rid of the workers. The Master of Metropolis agrees. First, Rotwang needs to steal some human souls for his **robots**.

With his robot Maria standing by, Dr. Rotwang tells the Master of his vision for the future — robot workers that make no mistakes and never tire.

MACHINE WOMAN

Maria is the hero of *Metropolis*. She tells the workers to change the world peacefully. Rotwang kidnaps Maria and makes his machine steal some of her soul for the robot. The real Maria is not harmed, but all her work is ruined by the mean robot version of Maria.

The robot gets the workers to wreck the machines that not only run the city, but also take care of their own homes. They remember this too late! Their homes and their children are lost!

Do you ever feel like machines are controlling your life? Try to imagine a life without any machines at all. Would it be better to do *everything* yourself?

A little bit of Maria's soul is sucked into the robot to give it life. Even a mean monster like the robot Maria needs a bit of humanity to make it work!

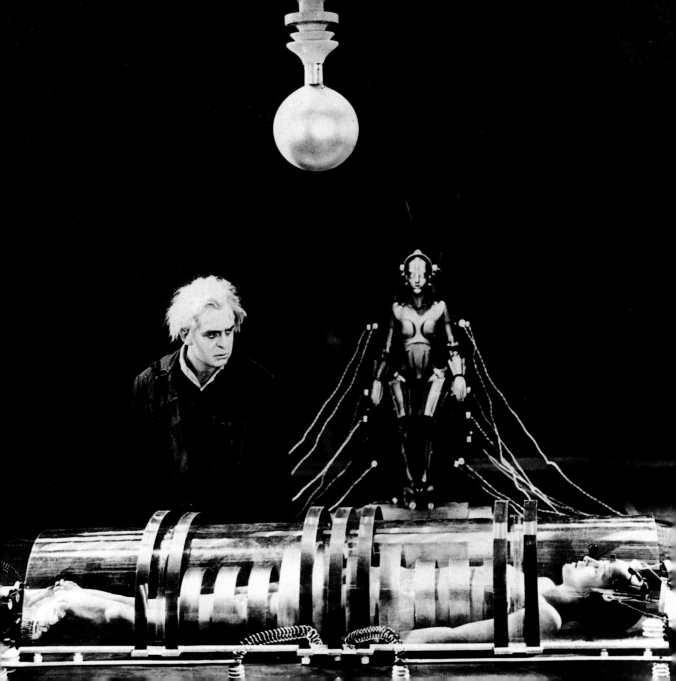

ANTI-DROID

In the movie *Bladerunner*, **androids** are robotic slaves that do the work humans choose not to do.

Six androids learn that all androids are "fixed" — that they deactivate when their "expiry" date is up. This way, the androids cannot break down with age. Also, in theory, they will not have time to learn real feelings. Without emotions, their creators think, an android could never want to rule the world.

In *Bladerunner*, most androids never even know they are not human. Do you think just having emotions causes a person to want to rule the world?

In *Bladerunner*, this super-fast, super-strong android looks for his maker to learn why androids have to die. How do you think he'll feel when he finds out?

OUR MONSTERS, OUR SELVES?

Some types of machines in our world handle nuclear waste, cook dinner, wash dishes, or answer the phone. They do things we cannot do, or things we just don't want to do.

We expect our creations to be faster and smarter than we are. Sometimes they are; sometimes they are not. Experts say it will be many, many years before we make anything as complex as a person — no matter what materials we use.

In movies, manmade people often turn out to be monsters. Are we afraid, deep down, that they might turn out to behave . . . just like we do?

The android Cog was made by researcher Rodney Brooks to study how humans learn. Cog is not a monster robot. He's a teacher and a student in one.

MORE TO READ, VIEW, AND LISTEN TO

Books (Nonfiction)   *Artificial Intelligence: Robotics and Machine Evolution.* David Jefferis
(Crabtree)
Monsters (series). Janet Perry and Victor Gentle (Gareth Stevens)
Movie Monsters. Tom Powers (Lerner)
Robots: Your High Tech World. Gloria Skurzynski (Simon & Schuster)
The Woman Who Created Frankenstein: A Portrait of Mary Shelley.
Janet Harris (HarperCollins)

Books (Activity)   *How to Draw Robots and Aliens.* Janet Cook (EDC)
Make-up Monsters. Marcia Lynn Cox (Grosset & Dunlap)
Monsters and Extraterrestrials. Draw, Model, and Paint (series).
Isidro Sánchez (Gareth Stevens)
More Halloween Howls: Riddles That Come Back to Haunt You.
Giulio Maestro (Dutton's Children's Books)

Books (Fiction)   *Frankenstein.* Mary Wollstonecraft Shelley (Dover)
Frankenstein. (Wishbone Classics, No. 7). Michael Burgan
(HarperCollins)
Monster Soup and Other Spooky Poems. Dylis Evans (Scholastic)
My Robot Buddy. Alfred Slote (HarperCollins)
My School Is Worse Than Yours. Tom Toles (Viking)
Norby and the Terrified Taxi. Janet Asimov (Walker)

Videos (Fiction)   *Abbott and Costello Meet Frankenstein.* (Universal Studios)
Bladerunner. (Warner Bros.)
Dr. Who — The Robots of Death. (Twentieth-Century Fox)
Forbidden Planet. (MGM/UA Studios)
Frankenstein. (Universal Studios)
The Island of Dr. Moreau. (New Line Studios)
Mary Shelley's Frankenstein. (Columbia/Tristar Studios)
Metropolis. (Jef Films)

WEB SITES

If you have your own computer and Internet access, great! If not, most libraries have Internet access. Go to your library and enter the word *museums* into the library's preferred search engine. See if you can find a museum web page that has exhibits on medical science, cloning, bioengineering, genetics, or artificial intelligence. If any of these museums are close by, you can visit them in person!

The Internet changes every day, and web sites come and go. We believe the sites we recommend here are likely to last, and give the best and most appropriate links for our readers to pursue their interest in robotics, androids, medical discoveries, clones, and other creatures made by scientists and engineers.

www.ajkids.com

This is the junior *Ask Jeeves* site – a great research tool.

Some questions to *Ask Jeeves Kids*:
- *Where can I learn about robots?*
- *Where can I learn about Orson Welles?*
- *Where can I find information about mechanical body parts?*
- *What is cybernetics?*
- *Who makes androids?*

You can also type in words and phrases with a "?" at the end, for example,
- *Animal electricity?*
- *Cyborgs?*

http://nyelabs.kcts.org/f_index.html

Bill Nye is a scientist who has a public television show. This is his web site "lab." Go have a look around! Nyelabs is totally awesome, but more challenging than the other sites we have listed.

www.yahooligans.com

This is the junior Yahoo! home page. Click on Science & Nature. Then click on one of the listed topics (such as Animals, Computer Science, Living Things, Machines, Museums and Exhibits, and Physical Sciences) for more links. Or, click on one of the links (such as ScienceBob.com, NPR Science Friday Kids Connection, The Lab, Evidence: The True Witness, Kinetic City Cyber Club) to see what's really cool there. You can also search for more information by typing a word in the Yahooligans search engine. Some words to try are: *androids, artificial intelligence, clones, cybernetics, electricity, genetics, molecules,* and *robots*.

GLOSSARY

You can find these words on the pages listed. Reading a word in a sentence helps you understand it even better.

androids (AN-droydz) — robots that look and act very much like humans 18, 20

artificial (are-tih-FISH-uhl) — made by humans; not natural 6, 10

cardio defibrillator (CAR-dee-oh dee-FIB-rih-lay-ter) — an electrical device that sometimes helps start a person's heart after a heart attack 10

cyborg (SIGH-borg) — a human made up in part of computer pieces and machinery 6

deactivate (dee-AK-tiv-ate) — turn off 4, 18

electricity (ee-lek-TRIS-uh-tee) — a flow of electrons (tiny particles that have a negative electrical charge) that delivers power 8, 10

electronic (ee-lek-TRON-ik) — having to do with electrons, or relating to a device that works because of electron movement 6

organic (or-GAN-ik) — having to do with living material (animal and plant parts), whether alive or dead 6

robotic (roh-BAH-tik) — made of machine parts 6, 18

robots (ROH-botz) — machines that do complicated jobs 14, 16, 20

tissue (TIH-shoo) — flesh 12

transplant (TRANZ-plant) — a piece of body tissue or an organ that has been moved from one place to another 12

INDEX

WILDER BRANCH LIBRARY
7140 E. SEVEN MILE RD.
DETROIT, MI 48234